How This Book Got Red

We hang out in **treetops** to sunbathe and hide from snow leopards.

How This Book Got Red

Words by
Margaret Chiu
Greanias

Pictures by
Melissa Iwai

sourcebooks
jabberwocky

To Katie, Jack, and Alex: The future is yours to write.
—MCG
For my son, Jamie.
—MI

Text © 2023 by Margaret Chiu Greanias
Illustrations © 2023 by Melissa Iwai
Cover and internal design © 2023 by Sourcebooks

The illustrations in this book were created with watercolor, colored pencils, and digital tools.

Published by Sourcebooks Jabberwocky, an imprint of Sourcebooks Kids
P.O. Box 4410, Naperville, Illinois 60567-4410
(630) 961-3900
sourcebookskids.com

Cataloging-in-Publication Data is on file with the Library of Congress.

Source of Production: Leo Paper, Heshan City, Guangdong Province, China
Date of Production: March 2023
Run Number: 5030705

Printed and bound in China.
LEO 10 9 8 7 6 5 4 3 2 1

Red and Gee were looking through books when Gee spied the perfect one. "LOOK, A BOOK ABOUT PANDAS!" he said.

Red's eyes went wide. "I'm a panda!"
"You are."

"And *you're* a panda."
"I am."

"A book about us?"

Red hopped from
paw to paw.

"This will be better
than bamboo
bubble tea!"

They took the book to the tree house.
"Ready for an un-bear-lievable
read?" Gee asked.
The pandas dove in.

They read page...

after page...

after page...

until they reached The End.

HOW COULD A BOOK ABOUT PANDAS TOTALLY LEAVE OUT *RED* PANDAS?!?

"I'm writing my *own* book about pandas." Red got out a pen and paper.

Gee made space at the table. "You should!"

Red wrote...
And erased.

Wrote...
And erased.

Wrote...

And wailed, "Why does nothing feel good enough?!"
"How about a change of scenery?" Gee suggested.

BOOK EMPORIUM
书店

PANDAS EVERYWHERE!

GROCERY

PANDAS EVERYWHERE!

P is for PANDA
B is for BAMBOO

The New Panda

Panda's First Birthday

HUSH! PAN

HUG ME
I'M A PANDA!

T TODAY!
ANDAS
ERYWHERE!

PANDAS EVERYWHERE!

3:00 P.M.
BOOK Signing

Except everywhere they went, Red noticed how red pandas were missing from everything. She felt like the smallest speck of dust.
"Who am I *kidding*?" she said, crumbling. "No one wants to read about *red* pandas."
"That's not true!" Gee said.

"Then how do you explain *this*?" Red asked.

There were all kinds of books about all kinds of giant pandas...
But not *one* about *red* pandas. The facts were black and white.
"Eep!" Gee squeaked. "I see what you mean."

"I don't know *what* I was thinking," Red mumbled.
She tossed her book in the bin.

Bamboo bubble tea couldn't cheer Red up.

Neither could forest bathing.

Or pushing on trees.

It was no use.

On their way back...

What's going on?

Gee gave his friend a nudge.
Red's heart thumpity thumped. "...Because
I didn't think anyone wanted to read about
red pandas?"

"Told you!" Gee said.
"Well..." Red said.
"I guess I have a book to finish!"

With new energy, she poured her soul onto page...

after page...

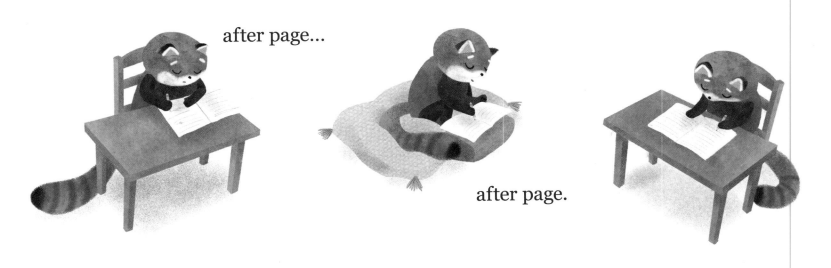

after page.

Gee illustrated.

"Uh, Gee? Red pandas can't fly," Red said.

"I thought this was a superhero book," Gee replied.

Well, we *can* climb down trees headfirst.

Whaaaaa???

"We *are* pretty amazing."
Red sat a little straighter.

At last...
"We're done!" Red read the finished book. "Oh Gee, it's *me*. And it's *PERFECT*!" she shouted from the treetops.

They put the book where *everyone* could see it.

Red hoped other red pandas would see themselves in the book.
But if they didn't...
maybe they'd be inspired to write their own.

"Someday there will be all kinds of books about all kinds of
red pandas," Red said.

There would be something perfect...

for everyone.

Giant pandas were named after US, but people still call us lesser pandas, firefoxes, and cat-bears.

We do a **wiggle dance** to mark our territory.

We stand up and **huff-quack** to say **"Stay away!"**

Our **tails** double as **blankets.**

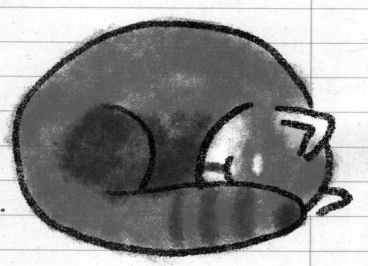

Margaret Chiu Greanias is not a red panda, but when she was growing up she also did not see herself in many books. She is the author of the picture books *Hooked On Books*, *Amah Faraway*, and *Maximillian Villainous*. The daughter of Taiwanese immigrants, she lives in the San Francisco Bay Area with her husband and three children.

Melissa Iwai is an award-winning children's book author and illustrator of *Soup Day*, *Pizza Day*, *Dumplings for Lili*, and the I Can Read series *Gigi and Ojiji*. She has illustrated over forty picture books during her career. Melissa lives in Brooklyn with her husband and Shiba Inu daughter, Nikki. She has a soft spot for cuteness with attitude, and red pandas and black-and-white pandas always make her smile.